2061: Photographing Mars

written by Richard Brightfield

illustrated by Vincent Nguyen

McGraw-Hill School Division

New York   Farmington

Mars at Last

After a two-week trip, Pam finally landed on Mars. As she walked into the terminal, her legs felt wobbly. On the Mars flight, she had spent four hours a day in artificial gravity—but even so, she wasn't used to standing up. With a quick glance at the screen of her computer goggles, she reminded herself of the names of her hosts.

She went to the cafeteria in the terminal, where she would meet them. It was crowded with people of all ages. Some of the food was brought in from Earth, but Pam was eager to try the vegetables grown in greenhouses on Mars. The cucumbers were cool and fresh, the carrots sweet and crisp.

As she was finishing her meal, a boy and girl about her age came up to her table. "You must be Pam," said the boy.

"Kenzo," replied Pam, "it's so nice to meet you. And you must be Val," Pam added, turning to the girl. "I'm really glad you can help me with my photo project. Were you born here on Mars?"

"Yes, and so was Kenzo," said Val, "—that's why we wanted to be your partners. A lot of our friends remember Earth, but we've never been there."

"Pam, you must have read about Mars on your trip over. Do you know what you want to photograph?"

"Well, I definitely want to see the face in Cydonia," Pam said.

Kenzo and Val exchanged a glance. "Oh, that," Kenzo said, "it's just a big pile of rocks. There are so many interesting things on Mars, we wonder why people come all the way here just to see *that*."

Pam was surprised, but she said politely, "I'm sure you're right, but I promised my class I'd photograph it."

Pam sat talking with her new friends in the cafeteria. She could tell they had a lot of affection for Earth, where their parents were born. They were both training in a high-gravity gym to travel to Earth. Earth's gravity was much stronger than Mars's, so they had to prepare carefully to avoid injury.

"Well, you'll need to pick up your Mars suit," said Kenzo. "Your computer probably sent your size, but the suit will have to be fitted." They went to a room in the terminal, where a technician carefully checked the suit.

"Perfect fit," the technician said. The special material would protect her from the thin atmosphere and from the threat of the sun's ultraviolet rays. The suit had a soft, clear helmet that went right over her goggles.

The three young people next walked to the garage. "Our school lent us a rover to show you around," said Kenzo.

"You can drive it yourself?" Pam asked, feeling jealous. "I won't be able to drive an Earth car until I'm 18."

"There's a lot less traffic here," Val said, laughing.

Pam attached the camera to her computer goggles. She photographed the terminal behind the rover and a huge dome far away to the right. The camera would store one hundred pictures on a disk and then transmit them to her classroom on Earth by satellite.

"That dome under construction over there is going to cover a new city," Val said. "They're digging a crater for the base. It's five miles across."

The Incredible Canyon

"When will we get to Cydonia?" Pam asked.

"In a while," Kenzo said. "There are some other things we would like to show you first—like the largest natural feature on any planet in our solar system. You can see it from Earth with a telescope."

"We'll be there tomorrow," Val said. "We'll stay overnight in a way-station. They are spread all around the planet. We can get something to eat, get more air, and refuel the rover with hydrogen."

As the sun dropped low in the sky, a large cube appeared in the distance. It was starkly white against the rust-colored surface of the planet. When they arrived at the cube, Val pressed a button in the rover, and an air-lock slid open at the cube's base.

Val parked *Quasar* and got out. "We can catch the sunset," she said.

They went outside and Pam began aiming her goggles all around, snapping pictures. The ground was covered with rocks in every shade of red, pink, and orange, and some had tiny crystals in them that sparkled like jewels.

Sunset looked completely different from Mars. Its atmosphere turned the rays crimson and orange, with pale greens mixed in. Then it was suddenly dark. The stars were brilliant overhead. There was a bright object that looked about half the size of Earth's moon moving across the sky.

"That's our potato-shaped moon, Phobos," Kenzo said, pointing up. "It's much smaller than Earth's moon, but it's a lot closer to us. Deimos, our other moon, is so small it looks like a star."

7

Pam, Kenzo, and Val each had a small room in the way-station. They started out again the next day. "What is the climate like?" Pam asked. "I can't feel anything though my Mars suit."

"It's summer, and right now"—she checked a dial in the rover—"it's 70 degrees Fahrenheit. If it were winter, it would be 60 to 90 degrees below zero."

"Could we get lost out here?" Pam asked.

"No chance," Val said, "there aren't many roads, but we have methods of navigating. The rovers have detailed maps and can find their way even in a dust storm. We can also track our location by satellite."

Just before noon, Val drove off the road and got out. "Don't get too close to the edge," she said, "it's a three-mile drop to the bottom!"

"Three miles?" Pam repeated.

"That's right," Val said, "Earth's Grand Canyon is small compared to this. This canyon is three times as deep, and much longer—it would stretch from New York to Los Angeles. It's named *Valles Marineris*, or Mariner Valley, after the first space probe from Earth almost a hundred years ago. We're at the western end, so it's only about 60 miles across, but in some places it's 250 miles across."

"I've seen movies of it, but seeing it in person is still amazing," Pam said. She took dozens of photographs while clinging to a rock safely back from the edge. "Is it true that it was formed by water? It's so dry here."

9

"Millions of years ago, Mars was much warmer and had rivers, lakes, maybe oceans," Kenzo answered, "but now there's only ice near the poles."

"The canyon's sides have layers of sediment left by water," Val added. "Also, there are thousands of water-carved channels leading into it."

"My mother says that the rivers and lakes will come back one day," Kenzo said, "when Mars is *terraformed*—made more like Earth, with a thicker atmosphere and a warmer climate. She's a scientist working on terraforming," he said with pride, "—you'll meet her where we're going next."

"To Cydonia?" Pam asked.

"We'll get there, but first we're going to the top of the tallest mountain in the solar system."

The Tallest Mountain

"It will take us a couple of days to get there," Val said. "We have to go around the western end of the canyon. There are several way-stations along the way. It's a very popular route. *Olympus Mons* is the most photographed place on Mars."

"I thought the face was the most photographed," Pam said.

"There you go with the face again," Kenzo said.

"Do you think it's true that there was intelligent life on Mars ages ago that built the face?" Pam asked.

"No way," said Kenzo. "Cydonia is just a pile of rocks."

For the next two days, Val, Kenzo, and Pam explored ancient river beds and craters. Pam sent photos back to her class, and got return messages saying how much everyone liked them.

"Are we close to the mountain?" Pam asked.

"We're going up the side of it now," Val said. "The base is 300 miles wide, but the slope is so gentle you hardly notice it. It will take most of the day to get there. This mountain, *Olympus Mons*, is three times higher than Earth's Mount Everest," Kenzo said.

Finally they reached the top and looked into a deep crater. Looking away from the mountain, Pam could see the curve of the planet, and in the other direction, the crater stretched for fifty miles. There was a scattering of buildings on the floor of the crater ten thousand feet below.

A road was cut into the sloping ridge of the crater down to the bottom. When they got there, they all went to the lava-proof building in which Kenzo's mother worked. She already knew Val, and Kenzo introduced Pam.

"We're testing to see if there's any volcanic activity still going on under the mountain," Kenzo's mother said. "If it became an active volcano, it could spew out carbon dioxide to build up the Martian atmosphere."

Kenzo's mother explained more about terraforming to Pam. Then she asked her son, "Where are you going from here?"

"We're taking Pam up to Cydonia," Kenzo said.

"That's a long trip! Your vacation is over in two days," she reminded them, "you'd better take the rocket."

Finally, Cydonia

With his mother's small rocket, the trip to
Cydonia was only a couple of hours. Just before
they landed, Pam caught a glimpse of the "face"
from above. Nearby, a small building housed the
Cydonia information center and gift shop, which
sold maps, souvenirs, and T-shirts. Pam bought
gifts for her family while Kenzo rented a go-cart.

"The cliff should be our first stop," Kenzo said,
"from there we can get an overview of the area."

He drove the car to the cliff—a wall about a
hundred feet high and three miles long.

They left the go-cart at one end of the cliff and walked up a path to the top. Pam was having fun taking photographs. "This is amazing!" she said. "Do you really think nature formed this?"

"My theory is that this whole area was once covered with a mile-deep layer of mineral matter," Val said. "Then, over millions of years, the wind blew most of it away, leaving a bunch of large mounds."

The famous "face" was a plateau about two miles long and two thousand feet high. From the ground, it had the aspect of a somewhat flattened face.

Later, they inspected a mile-high rock structure that looked like a pyramid with five sides. Then they moved on to a group of three-sided rocks that seemed to have been arranged around an open central area.

Pam photographed them all. "So, what do you think?" Kenzo asked her. "Were there ancient Martians?"

"Well, all this doesn't look like an accident, but you never know," she added quickly. "I certainly understand why people are so interested in this place, though," she said, taking a few final pictures. "You know what, a flight to Earth leaves tomorrow, and I'm supposed to be on it!"

"No problem," Kenzo said, "the space terminal is less than half a day's trip in the rocket."

"You've both been great," Pam said, "I couldn't have completed my photo project without you. I'm sorry to leave Mars. Do you think you'll ever come to Earth?"

"I hope we can, Pam," Val answered, "I hear it's pretty interesting there, too!"